VENICE TRAVEL GUIDE FOR KIDS

Creating Memories for Children in
Venice, An Adventure for Kids in Venice

By:

PAUL J. SHIPP

TABLE OF CONTENT

Chapter 4: "Treats and Treasures: Venetian Delights"

- Culinary exploration of Venetian treats like gelato and cicchetti
- Kid-friendly recipes inspired by traditional Venetian dishes

Chapter 5: "Islands of Wonders: Murano and Burano"

- Discover the unique charm of Murano's glass blowing and Burano's colorful houses
- Engaging activities for kids to appreciate the artistry of these islands

• Conclusion

Embark on a Venetian adventure filled with history, mystery, and delicious delights, making every moment in Venice unforgettable for young explorers!

Bonus: TRAVEL PLAN

INTRODUCTION

Hey, aspiring adventurers! As we set sail through the enchanted canals of Venice, a city that seems to float like a dream on the glistening Adriatic waters, be ready for an incredible voyage. Every page of this Venice Travel Guide for Kids is a passport to an amazing world where art, history, and adventure all come together in a vibrant symphony of stories.

Learn how Venice was constructed on water and the reason gondolas glide so elegantly down the Grand Canal as we explore the narrow waterways.

Visit the Venice Carnival's mask-wearing characters and discover the mysteries of St Mark's Basilica, whose mosaics depict historical events dating back hundreds of years. This tour offers family-friendly activities such as building your own gondola and sampling delectable Venetian sweets.

So gather your curiosity, don your explorer's hat, and come along for a unique trip across Venice that will include games, stories, and all the charm that makes this city so special for children of all ages. ¡Tu aspetta, Venezia! (Venice is on its way!)

1

Introduction to the Magical City of Venice

Venice is a city unlike any other, a timeless masterpiece that enthralls everyone who wanders its winding alleys. It is perched upon a network of canals, where gondolas glide smoothly over waterways. Get ready to be taken to a world where romance, art, and history come together to create a symphony of magic as soon as you set foot in this floating metropolis.

Venice, sometimes referred to as the "City of Canals," is a dreamlike place where dreams and reality coexist harmoniously.

Its distinct attractiveness comes from the lack of roadways in favor of a system of canals that are crossed by recognisable gondolas and dotted with arched arches that evoke memories of bygone eras. Venice appears as the mist from the lake rises in the morning, revealing charming squares and an old façade.

Venice's major waterway, the Grand Canal, acts as a liquid conduit through the city's center. With its row of lavish mansions and vibrant structures that appear to rise out of the water, it provides a cinematic introduction to the charm of this floating metropolis.

The Grand Canal is transformed into a romantic water procession as the sun sets, illuminating the water with a warm glow. Gondoliers expertly navigate their boats beneath historic structures.

With centuries of history revealed in each piazza and calle, Venice is a living museum. With its stunning Byzantine mosaics and commanding view of St. Mark's Square, the imposing St. Mark's Basilica beckons visitors to travel back in time. The Doge's Palace is a nearby example of Venetian majesty and power.

This overview of the enchanted city of Venice sets the scene for an adventure through tiny lanes, over arched bridges, and across glistening canals. Venice promises an experience that goes beyond the ordinary with its magical atmosphere and rich cultural tapestry—a trip into a city where the past and present dance in harmony, producing a place that stays in the hearts of everyone who is fortunate enough to explore its treasures.

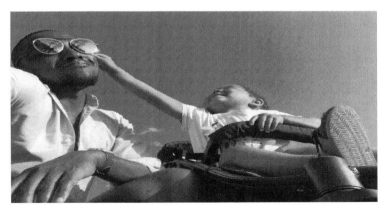

The story of how Venice was built on water and its famous canals

Venice's architectural miracle, which defies convention, is a story of inventiveness created out of need. The city was established in the fifth century, and its distinctive base is made up of 118 islands that are connected by a system of waterways. Rather from being a hindrance, this complex underwater maze grew to be Venice's lifeblood, defining its character and giving it an unmatched aura of enchantment.

Marshy lagoons and tidal waves presented a difficult environment for

Venice's builders, but instead of struggling against it, they embraced the water. To build a strong foundation for the city, wooden pilings were pushed far into the swampy area. Made of robust larch wood, these pilings were driven through the soft soil and into the more stable clay beneath, providing Venice with a solid base that defied the odds.

Originally, the Grand Canal—the city's principal thoroughfare—was a saltwater lagoon. This natural stream was transformed into a busy river by Venetian engineers and architects over many centuries.

Palaces that highlight Venice's opulence and luxury during its golden age along its banks.

The renowned Venetian canals are the city's lifeblood, serving as more than just transit corridors. The canals, which are woven throughout Venice, are crossed by a fleet of graceful gondolas and vaporettos, defining daily life with a flowing cadence. Every canal connects the city's lively neighborhoods and reflects the history of the city.

The tale of how Venice's renowned canals and floating city were created is proof of how resilient and adaptive people can be.

It tells the story of a city that turned its obstacles into artistic opportunities to create a one-of-a-kind urban masterpiece where water serves as both a source of inspiration and a barrier. Venice, with its graceful floating architecture, continues to be a symbol of the spirit of architectural innovation and the peaceful coexistence of man and environment.

3

Explore the iconic gondolas and their role in Venetian transportation

The famous gondolas float elegantly through the heart of Venice, where the maze-like network of canals creates a watery tapestry that represents not only elegance and history but also Venetian style. These sleek, black boats are more than just modes of transportation; as they move through the city's watery alleys, they whisper stories from centuries past with their characteristic iron prow and curved form.

The gondola is an exquisite example of form and function, built to glide gracefully through Venice's winding, narrow canals. Because of the gondola's distinctive asymmetry, which is created by combining eight different types of wood, one gondolier can expertly move the boat ahead with just one oar. Every stroke is evidence of the age-old methods that have been passed down through the ancestors of Venetian gondoliers.

Gondolas have been an essential part of Venetian transit for generations, despite the fact that tourists may associate them with romantic trips.

For the Venetian elite, gondolas were the main means of transit in a city where canals are the main roadway. These days, they provide both locals and tourists with a leisurely and picturesque ride that winds through tiny canals and passes under famous bridges.

These boats' expert captains, known as gondoliers, are storytellers in addition to navigators. They tell stories of Venice's rich past as they steer their gondolas, exposing obscure passages and little-known events that enhance the story of the city.

Examining the recognisable gondolas exposes a timeless dance between tradition and modernity more than just a means of transportation. These graceful boats transport the spirit of Venice, a city where every gondola ride is an adventure through romance and history, as they thread through the intricate network of waterways.

Visit majestic landmarks like St. Mark's Basilica and the Doge's Palace

Saint. Mark's Basilica and the Doge's Palace are two magnificent buildings that serve as guardians of the city's rich legacy in the center of Venice, where the whispers of history resonate across large squares and antique façade. By taking tourists on a trip through time, these architectural wonders reveal the mysteries of Venetian strength, faith, and creative splendor.

A Masterwork of Mosaics: St. Mark's Basilica

St. Mark's Basilica, the glistening jewel of St. Mark's Square, is evidence of the Byzantine impact on the city. Visitors are greeted by its elaborate facade, which is decorated with golden mosaics and fine carvings, into a hallowed area where every surface is a work of artistic genius. Enter to see a world of glistening mosaics that portray biblical stories, elaborate marble flooring, and the renowned Pala d'Oro, a golden altarpiece that dazzles with precious gems. St. Mark's Basilica is not just a religious sanctuary; it is a living testament to the cultural fusion that defines Venice.

Doge's Palace: The Meeting Place of Opulence and Power

Venetian political power is seated in the Doge's Palace, which is close to St. Mark's Basilica. With its beautiful tracery and pink facade, this magnificent Gothic masterpiece emanates a sense of regal grandeur. Walk across the famous Bridge of Sighs, which links the palace to the old prisons, and discover luxurious rooms filled with Venetian painterly masterpieces. The complex web of justice, luxury, and governance that moulded the Venetian Republic's history is revealed by the Doge's Palace.

Experiencing these magnificent sites is more than simply a sightseeing excursion; it's a voyage through Venice's political and cultural fabric. With their enduring beauty and historical significance, St. Mark's Basilica and the Doge's Palace provide a window into a world where faith, art, and power converged to create the enchanting city of Venice.

4

Culinary exploration of Venetian treats like gelato and cicchetti

A haven for foodies, Venice is a city of meandering canals and historic beauty that offers an exquisite selection of delicacies that entice the senses. Explore the charming alleyways while indulging in a culinary journey with two quintessential Venetian treats: gelato and cicchetti.

A Symphony of Flavours: Gelato Bliss

The seductive sound of gelato, a frozen treat that goes beyond dessert, beckons visitors to Venice's sun-kissed streets.

A kaleidoscope of flavors awaits you when you enter a typical gelateria, ranging from the traditional stracciatella to exotic fruits and rich chocolate. The essence of Italian gelato creativity is encapsulated in Venetian gelato, a creamy symphony. Savor every bite as you stroll along the canals, allowing the rich flavors and velvety texture to carry you away to another world.

Cicchetti: Tiny Bits, Massive Flavor

The culture of cicchetti is king in the center of Venice. Similar to Spanish tapas, these little tasty morsels highlight the depth of Venetian cuisine.

Enter a bacaro, a classic Venetian wine bar, and savor a mouthwatering selection of cicchetti, which include fried treats, flavorful meatballs and exquisite seafood crostini. Each bite is a taste of the region, showcasing the culinary inventiveness and seafaring history of the city. When you enjoy your cicchetti in a social setting with locals, pair it with a glass of Venetian wine or a spritz.

Discovering the delights of Venetian cuisine, such as gelato and cicchetti, is a celebration of the city's diverse culinary culture rather than merely a culinary excursion.

Every mouthful and scoop extends an invitation to savor the unique flavors that make Venice a destination where every meal is a moment to cherish.

VENICE TRAVEL GUIDE FOR KIDS

Kid-friendly recipes inspired by traditional Venetian dishes

Young cooks, join us for a culinary journey influenced by the tastes of Venice! With these kid-friendly recipes that encapsulate the spirit of classic Venetian fare, discover the beauty of Italian cuisine.

Pasta Boat Adventure in a Gondola:
Try making your own pasta gondolas with this fun recipe. Select your preferred pasta shape and feel free to express your creativity. Each pasta boat becomes a work of art when colorful vegetables are threaded onto toothpicks to create sails.

As your culinary creations go on a delectable journey, watch these gondolas sail into a sea of tomato sauce.

Cicchetti Capers:

These bite-sized sweets will allow you to introduce the Venetian custom of cicchetti into your kitchen. Add fresh basil, mozzarella cubes, and diced tomatoes to a mixture. For Cicchetti Capers, skewer these delicious combos onto toothpicks. These little morsels are ideal for a picnic-style dinner or family feast because they are full of flavour.

Gelato Pops for the Venetian Carnival:

Gelato pops may turn the excitement of the Venetian Carnival into frozen enjoyment. Scoop out your favourite gelato flavors and roll them with shredded chocolate, broken biscuits or seasonal sprinkles. For a treat reminiscent of a carnival, insert popsicle sticks and freeze. These Gelato Pops are a delightful homage to the exuberance that permeates Venice's streets during carnival season.

Canal-side Gondolas for Fruit:

Create a tasty and nutritious snack that is reminiscent of Venice's canals.

Cut pears or apples into boat shapes, then coat them with cream cheese. Let your fruit gondolas sail into a sea of yogurt or honey for dipping by using thin pretzel sticks as oars. It's a novel approach to infuse your snack time with the spirit of Venice's waterways.

These kid-friendly dishes make cooking a fun adventure while introducing young cooks to the bright flavours of Venetian cuisine. So get your ingredients, don your aprons, and let's start exploring the kitchen! Good Food! (Savour your food!)

5

Discover the unique charm of Murano's glass blowing and Burano's colorful houses

Beyond Venice's picturesque canals are the two enchanted islands of Murano and Burano, which add a distinct chapter to the lagoon's history. The charming Venetian gems of Murano, known for its mastery of glassblowing, and Burano, with its kaleidoscope of colourful dwellings, encourage visitors to discover the artistic marvels and lively charm that characterise them.

Murano's Mastery of Glassblowing:
From Venice, take a quick vaporetto ride to Murano, where glassblowing is a centuries-old craft that has been refined. Enter the island's workshops and watch as expert craftspeople create stunning works of art out of molten glass. Murano's glass gems, which range from delicate figurines to elaborate chandeliers, are a testament to the generations-long tradition of artistry. Young visitors can marvel at the captivating dance of flames and glass, getting a close-up look at the magic that transforms unfinished objects into glittering masterpieces.

The glass symphony in Murano is a visual feast that transports guests to an infinitely creative universe.

Burano's Painted Dreams: Just a short boat journey from Murano, the island of Burano is home to a kaleidoscope of colors. Here, homes have vivid colors that appear out of the usual. Take a stroll down Burano's winding streets, where every house has a unique color scheme that conveys a story. There is a legend that the brightly coloured cottages aided fishermen in navigating through the fog to return home.

Whether accurate or not, the end product is an amazing visual show that fascinates both adults and young adventurers. Explore Burano's lace stores, sample the cuisine, and, of course, take pictures of the rainbow-hued homes that turn this island into a living canvas to really appreciate its allure.

Exploring the glassblowing craftsmanship of Murano and the vibrant homes of Burano is not only a voyage, but It's an exploration of the distinct artistry and lively spirit that characterize these islands of Venetian culture.

Those who are fortunate enough to visit Murano's glass studios and Burano's streets will never forget the tale of ingenuity and beauty that is revealed at every turn and leaves a lasting impression on their hearts.

Engaging activities for kids to appreciate the artistry of these islands

The tour becomes a hands-on excursion for young travellers eager to discover the delights of Murano's glassblowing and Burano's colourful residences, stimulating creativity and respect for these Venetian islands' creative treasures.

The Glass Adventure of Murano:

Bring children to visit Murano's glassblowing workshops, where molten glass and fire combine to produce a breathtaking show. Make this an interactive experience by setting up a little glassblowing workshop for the kids. Children can shape and mould their glass creations, which might include a fanciful figurine or a small vase, with the assistance of expert artisans. Through this hands-on activity, children may experience the creativity directly and get the creative confidence they need to appreciate Murano's glass craftsmanship for the rest of their lives.

Burano's Vibrant Painting:

Burano's rainbow-colored homes provide a vivid setting for creative experimentation. Give them a paintbox, some colours, and a tiny canvas so they can draw the kaleidoscope of colours that decorate Burano's streets. With this painting exercise, kids can express their creativity and create a unique interpretation of the island's charm. It turns into a fun art project. What was the outcome? a collection of miniature works of art that capture the personality and vitality of Burano's vibrant homes.

Treasure Trove via Colors:

Organize a treasure hunt on Burano with a colour theme to transform discovery into an exciting adventure. Give them a list of colours to locate and have them match the colors of the houses. This interactive game teaches kids to notice and value the variety of colors around them in addition to adding excitement to the stroll through Burano's streets. The treasure hunt turns into a fun adventure that deepens their comprehension of Burano's distinct charm. Making kid-friendly activities out of exploring Murano and Burano strengthens their bond with these creative islands and helps them make lifelong memories.

Conclusion

It's time to say goodbye to the enchanted canals, colourful masks, and historical treasures that have weaved a tapestry of memories throughout our exploration of Venice as our Venetian adventure comes to an end. Every moment has been a pleasure, from making your own gondolas to enjoying gelato while taking in Burano's vibrant homes.

Young explorers, do not be alarmed, though, for the essence of Venice will endure in your hearts. No matter where your next adventure takes you, the stories of glassblowing in Murano,

The sounds of footsteps in St. Mark's Square, and the laughs exchanged over cicchetti will follow.

Recall that the world is a blank canvas just waiting to be discovered as you open the last page of this Venice travel guide for kids. Venice, all its classic beauty, has only been the tip of the iceberg. So, take the enchantment of Venice with you, imagine yourself riding a gondola, and use your memories of this wonderful city to spur on a myriad of future adventures. Ciao, little adventurers, and until we cross paths again in the world of wonders!

TRAVEL PLAN

✈ TRAVEL PLAN

Destination:	Duration:
Arrival:	Departure:

Hotel Address:
Transportation:

Day 1

Time	Activity
8:00 am	
12:00 nn	
1:00 pm	
3:00 pm	
7:00 pm	
10:00 pm	

 HAPPY TRAVEL

VENICE TRAVEL GUIDE FOR KIDS

✈ TRAVEL PLAN

Destination:	Duration:
Arrival:	Departure:

Hotel Address:
Transportation:

Day 1

Time	Activity
8:00 am	
12:00 nn	
1:00 pm	
3:00 pm	
7:00 pm	
10:00 pm	

HAPPY TRAVEL

VENICE TRAVEL GUIDE FOR KIDS

✈ TRAVEL PLAN

Destination:	Duration:
Arrival:	Departure:

Hotel Address:
Transportation:

Day 1

Time	Activity
8:00 am	
12:00 nn	
1:00 pm	
3:00 pm	
7:00 pm	
10:00 pm	

HAPPY TRAVEL

VENICE TRAVEL GUIDE FOR KIDS

✈ TRAVEL PLAN

Destination:	Duration:
Arrival:	Departure:

Hotel Address:
Transportation:

Day 1

Time	Activity
8:00 am	
12:00 nn	
1:00 pm	
3:00 pm	
7:00 pm	
10:00 pm	

HAPPY TRAVEL

VENICE TRAVEL GUIDE FOR KIDS

Made in the USA
Las Vegas, NV
13 March 2024